Ghost Hunters USA

By

Sandra Puckett

PUBLISHED BY REVELADE PUBLISHING
www.revelade.com

I dedicate this book to
my children, nieces, and nephews.

Christopher Puckett (CJ)
Joshua Kavanaugh
Zachary Kavanaugh
Chance Puckett
Trinity Puckett
Valerie Merseal
Jessica Merseal
Natalie Merseal
Ryan Nelson
Andrew Conaway
Tonya Conaway
Samantha Conaway
William Nickelson, Jr (Billy 5¢)
Brittany Nickelson

Ghost Hunters USA

Chapter 1

William Nickelson Jr. stood on the sidewalk that he had walked as a child, staring at the small elementary school that he once knew. Now a freshman in high school, his memories were faded just a bit…but was it really time that had faded those memories or was it his mind trying to give him some peace?

He remembered the first time he had walked the hallway alone in that school. All the other kids were sitting at their desks in their classrooms with their teachers watching over them as they worked on the problems for the day. He needed to visit the "little boys" room and was unable to wait until the designated restroom break, so his teacher allowed him to go on his own—after all, he *was* in third grade, clearly old enough to find his way to the bathroom and back with no problems…or so his teacher thought.

She was half right. It was on his way back from the bathroom when he saw it…a child…she had to have been a lost kinder-gartener. Why had her teacher let her go alone? Everyone knew a kindergartner would get lost in the maze they called school. All the pods looked alike, and kindergartners were unable to read well enough to know which pod was which. Anger swelled up inside him. How could her teacher be so heartless? She should've known the child would get lost.

He walked up to the little girl. The faint smell of smoke lingered on her clothes. *Her parents must be smokers*, he thought, glad that both of his parents had passed on that nasty habit. He gently touched the girl's shoulder. "It'll be okay. I'll take you to your classroom." The little girl looked up at him. And that's when he knew that she wasn't a lost kindergartner… not a lost child at all. She was a lost soul.

Empty, dark eyes stared into his.

His mouth opened, but only a small squeal came out, the scream caught in his throat. He was alone with the thing…all alone and unable to call for help. *Run,* he silently screamed at himself. *Turn and run!*

Chapter 2

"Billy!"

William jolted out of memory and turned. One of his cousins had arrived...Jessie Merseal. She slammed the car door shut and started toward him. He had called them all this time, every single one of his cousins. He usually didn't want so many people in the building when they were investigating, but with this one he wanted to make sure they had it covered. Well, that was his excuse to them. The truth was...he was really scared of this one. This one had inflicted an emotional, childhood scar that he couldn't shake. No matter what he did, he just couldn't shake it. "Where are Valerie, Natalie, and Ryan?" he asked as Jessie joined him on the sidewalk.

"They'll be here in a minute." She hugged him. "Nervous?"

He shrugged. "A little I guess."

"Don't be. We've seen worse than this." She smiled and nudged his arm. She knew his fear. She remembered how scared he was that day he saw the girl. She only wished that she could've experienced it too. She desperately tried to see it...constantly telling her teacher she needed to go to the bathroom or that she needed to go to the nurse—anything that would get her out of the classroom and into the hallway alone, but she guessed it didn't want to show itself to her. "Is Brittany coming?"

"Yeah, Andrew just left to pick her up. The equipment's already inside. We put it just inside the door. When everybody gets here, we'll pair up and set up and see what we get."

"How did they talk you into this?"

Billy looked into her eyes and took a deep breath. He felt foolish. Here he was a big, tough football player terrified of a small ghost child that dwelled inside a not-so-scary building. And there was Jessie, a short, thin girl unafraid of the thing living inside the school. "Well, the principal called me. He was desperate. The janitors refuse to clean the school until something is done."

"Did he try hiring someone else?"

"Yeah, but nobody will work here until this thing is gone."

"Well what do they expect *us* to do? We only prove the place is haunted. We're not ghost busters."

"I know. I made some calls. If we can get proof there's something here, there's a group of ghost hunters in Kansas City that'll try to get rid of it."

"Hey, we're here!" Natalie Merseal called out from the passenger seat of Valerie Merseal's Escort as they drove by and pulled into a parking spot. Ryan Nelson jumped out of the back passenger door no sooner than Valerie had shifted the car into park. He was eager to start his first ghost hunt.

Jessie walked over to the car to greet her sisters and brother.

"Good," Billy said to himself as the cavalry began to flow into the drive.

A red Caravan pulled up and parked beside Valerie's car. The driver's door opened and the side door slid back, and four cousins poured out...CJ Puckett, Joshua Kavanaugh, Zachary Kavanaugh, and Chance Puckett. A dark blue Chevy S10 parked beside the van, and Andrew Conaway and Brittany Nickelson climbed out. Arriving last, a teal Escort brought the remainder of the crew, Tonya Conaway and Samantha Conaway.

"Okay everybody, listen up." Billy cut off the hellos and how-are-yous. It was time to get down to business. It would be dark soon and they didn't need any mistakes on this one. The whole school administration was counting on him. He had started the ghost-hunting group, which led to him being the contact person, which led to people believing that the successes and failures of the group was his alone. "Brittany, Chance, Ryan, and Samantha since this is your first ghost hunt, you'll need to team up with someone that knows what they're doing. This is not a game. No playing around. We don't have much time before sunset and we need to get everything set up and ready to go. We're going to investigate this one from sunset until about four in the morning."

"Why so long on this one?" Valerie asked, brushing her short, brown hair back from her face. She was already tired, and it was barely five o'clock. She really wasn't up for this tonight, but she couldn't say no after hearing the desperation in Billy's voice. She had even cancelled a date with her boyfriend.

"We've got to get something tonight. I already know the school's haunted, but we've got to get proof," Billy replied.

"You've been avoiding this place since we've started investigating," Andrew said. "Are you sure you're ready for it?"

"No, but we're doing it anyway." They all knew he didn't want to do this one. He had refused it the whole year. Now he wished he had just faced his fear in the beginning and gotten it out of the way. Then he wouldn't be standing there in front of all his cousins feeling so foolish. They had all gone to this school, some of them were still attending, but none of them had seen the girl.

"Okay. Let's do it," CJ butted in. "Where's the stuff?"

"Just inside the door," Billy replied and led them to the door to his mom's classroom. She was a kindergarten teacher and not crazy about the ghost hunting thing, but supported her son's decision to investigate the paranormal. He turned the doorknob and everybody piled into the classroom. "This is a small school, but it's a big building compared to what we're used to investigating. Most of the activity has been in the older part of the building. The older kindergarten area and the first, second, and third grades area."

"That's the part that burned a long time ago," Zachary said.

"How do you know that?" Billy asked. The smell of smoke on the ghost child flashed in his mind.

"Research," Zachary replied. "Remember? I do the research on the buildings we investigate. Four kids died in that fire."

Chapter 3

Billy drew in a deep breath and turned his attention to the small pile of equipment sitting on the floor. That was more information than he wanted to know, but it was information that he needed to know. Actually, he should've consulted Zachary before they showed up to investigate. It must've been his subconscious not wanting to know just what they'd be dealing with. "CJ, you take Chance and Natalie and go to the entrance by the other kindergarten rooms. Set up a camcorder to record as much of that area as possible." He picked up a duffle bag and handed it to CJ.

CJ took the bag and led Chance and Natalie to their designated area. He unpacked the camcorder and set it up on a step facing one of the many entrances to the school and a kindergarten room then fished out the rest of the equipment from the bag. He handed Chance a walkie-talkie and Natalie a thermal scanner gun. He pocketed the digital voice recorder, pulled out the flashlight, and put the bag beside the camcorder.

"Are we gonna turn the lights out?" Chance asked, turning on the walkie-talkie.

"Yep," CJ answered.

"We can't tape in the dark," Chance said.

"This camcorder can record in the dark," CJ replied.

"Oh." Chance smiled. He was happy-go-lucky and didn't really know what he was getting himself into.

"Valerie," Billy said, "You take Joshua and Ryan and cover the first grade pod." He handed her a bag.

"Got it," Valerie said and led Joshua and Ryan to the entrance of the first grade pod. To their right and up the stairs was the foyer where CJ, Natalie, and Chance were setting up. "Stay here. I'll get a chair from one of the classrooms for the camcorder."

"Okay," Joshua said and watched as Valerie walked down the hall and into the first classroom to her left. He knelt down and pulled out a walkie-talkie and handed it to Ryan. "Here ya go."

Ryan took the walkie-talkie and turned it on.

Valerie returned with a chair and set the camcorder to cover the first grade pod's hallway.

Joshua fished out a thermal scanner gun, flashlight, and digital voice recorder. He handed the thermal scanner gun to Valerie.

"Check this out," Valerie said with a smile, pulling a digital camera from her purse.

"Where did you get that?" Joshua asked.

"Mom."

"Tonya, Zachary, and Brittany." Billy picked up another bag and handed it to Tonya. "You guys got the second grade pod."

"Cool." Tonya smiled.

At the second grade pod entrance, Tonya, Zachary, and Brittany could see Valerie, Joshua, and Ryan and the chair that Valerie had set their camcorder on.

"I'll get the chair," Zachary said, heading down the second grade hallway.

"Okay," Tonya said. She gave Brittany the walkie-talkie and retrieved the thermal scanner gun, digital voice recorder, flashlight, and camcorder and set them on the floor.

"Here we go." Zachary placed the chair at the entrance to the second grade pod. Tonya handed him the camcorder and he set it in the chair, positioning it to tape the second grade pod's hallway.

"Here." Tonya gave Zachary the thermal scanner gun and digital voice recorder. "I'm keeping the flash-light. I'm not gonna get left in the dark when we turn the lights out." She smiled, but wasn't joking. It had happened once before and ever since then she held the flashlight.

"Well, you know where you guys are going," Billy said to Andrew, Jessie, and Samantha.

Andrew nodded. "Third grade."

Jessie smiled. Billy had seen the ghost child near the third grade pod entrance. Maybe she would finally get to see it now.

Billy picked up a bag and handed it to Andrew then turned to grab the last bag, which held a flashlight, his mom's cell phone-she wanted to make sure he could call her if he got too scared, some extra batteries, and a walkie-talkie. "I'll walk down with you guys," he said, turning to an empty room. The hair stood up on the back of his neck. He was alone. His heart began to race. *It's okay,* he told himself. *The lights are all on. Just walk down to the third grade pod. They'll be there waiting for you.*

He squeezed the bag's handles in his left hand and turned to the door that led outside. *Great,* he thought. *It's already dark.* He locked the door. They didn't need anyone coming in on them. Then, taking a deep breath, he crossed the room and hesitantly stepped out into the school and started toward the third grade pod.

Chapter 4

"I can't believe they left me," Billy muttered to himself as he made his way down the long corridor. He wasn't afraid now. He could see Andrew, Jessie, and Samantha halfway down the hall, in front of the third grade pod, and Tonya, Zachary, and Brittany further down at the entrance to the second grade pod. And he knew that Valerie, Joshua, and Ryan were to the right and down the hall from Tonya's group, and that CJ, Chance, and Natalie were to the right of Valerie's group.

There was nothing for him to be afraid of. They were all, basically, together.

He continued to remind himself of that as he forced his legs to keep a slow steady pace. How would it look if he went running down the hallway to them? They'd all laugh at him.

"William," a whisper came from behind him.

He gasped. The hair stood up on the back of his neck. He spun around...to darkness.

The school was black.

Who turned the lights out? Billy wondered. *I'm the one that decides when the lights go out.* He put his back against the wall, dug into the duffel bag, and pulled out the flashlight. He shined it down the hall from where he just came. Nothing. He reached into the bag once again and got the walkie-talkie. "Who turned the lights out?" he asked angrily.

"Not us," Samantha answered.

"Not us," Ryan replied.

"Not us," Natalie said.

"Not us," came Brittany's voice.

"It's not funny," Billy announced to them over the walkie-talkie, now jogging toward Andrew, Jessie, and Samantha.

"Billy." The whisper was in his ear now.

Knowing he shouldn't, Billy shined the light over his left shoulder and stole a quick look.

Chapter 5

Billy saw nothing behind him, but he knew it was there. And it knew his name...it knew *him*. He imagined it at his back...reaching out to grab him—to pull him into eternal darkness. "It's here!" he yelled into the walkie-talkie.

"We're coming," each team had responded.

That made him feel a little better...until his flashlight went out. The batteries were dead. The thing had drained the batteries. He stared at the flashlights racing toward him. They would be his guides. He was almost there. He sighed. Then all was black again. The thing had drained their batteries, too. He couldn't see at all, but he could hear the sounds of his cousins' shoes smacking the floor as they ran toward him. They all had to stop running before they collided. "Stop! Stay where you are! I'll find you," he yelled down the hall. He put his hands out in front of him and slowly walked toward them. He wanted to run. His legs begged him to run, but he knew he had to remain calm. Things like that fed off of fear. And he didn't want it any stronger than it already was.

"Billy?" Valerie's voice broke the silence.

"Yeah," Billy answered.

"Don't you have the extra batteries?"

"Yeah…I do." How could he have forgotten? He put his duffel bag down on the floor and knelt beside it. He reached into the bag and felt for the batteries, found them, and took the flashlight apart. He took a deep breath as he slid the batteries into the flashlight and screwed it back together. He hoped the thing was gone…he didn't feel it behind him anymore. He turned the flashlight on. It shined on the bunch of ghost hunters standing twenty feet in front of him.

Billy rose to his feet and started for them. He watched them as he slowly closed the gap. Something was wrong. He stopped and searched their faces. They were all there. Watching him. Waiting for him. What was wrong? Was he just being paranoid?

"Billy," Brittany's voice came over his walkie-talkie, "where are you?"

"I'm right here," he answered, but not into the walkie-talkie.

"Billy, are you okay?" Brittany's voice came again from the walkie-talkie. She sounded a little concerned this time.

Billy pressed the button on the walkie-talkie and spoke into it. "I'm right here."

"Right where?" Brittany asked.

"Billy, quit playing around," Tonya's voice came from the walkie-talkie. "We're ready to get this thing going."

"Quit trying to scare me. I'm right here in front of you," he said.

"You're not in front of us," Tonya announced.

His hair stood on end as goose bumps rose from his head to his toes. He stared at the familiar faces. Were they really his cousins or something else?

"We're going for Billy," Tonya yelled down the brightly lit corridor to Valerie's group.

Valerie gave her the okay signal.

Tonya, Zachary, and Brittany ran down the hall.

"We'll be right back," Tonya said to Andrew as they passed by.

"Okay," Andrew answered. "Let us know if you need us," he called after them.

Tonya, Zachary, and Brittany raced into the kindergarten room where they had started.

"Where is he?" Brittany asked frantically. Tears swelled up in her eyes. There were times when he had made her mad; times when she had secretly said she didn't care about him, but that was the anger talking. He was her brother and she loved him. She didn't want anything to happen to him.

Tonya checked the door leading outside. "It's locked. Come on." She led her small group out of the room and stopped. "Billy, where are you?" she spoke into the walkie-talkie.

No answer.

"Look." Zachary pointed to his left at the gymnasium.

"Why would he go in there?" Tonya asked. "We never wander off alone."

They walked over to the doors and peered through the windows at the small beam of light shining in the darkness of the gym.

Tonya grabbed the back of Zachary's shirt. "You go first," she whispered, nudging him.

Zachary tossed a glance at her. *Just like a girl,* he thought. He slowly pulled the gym doors open and slipped inside with Tonya and Brittany at his back. "Billy?" Zachary called out as he felt the wall for the light switch.

Chapter 6

Billy slowly backed away from the group he had thought was his cousins. He kept the flashlight shined on them as he began to make his escape. He wasn't sure what he would do if they started for him. He guessed he'd have to turn and run and hope that he could get away.

"What are you doing?" Natalie's voice came from the group. "That thing is behind you. It's gonna get you."

Billy kept backing up. One behind him, many in front…he'd take his chances with the one.

Zachary found the light switch and pushed it up.
No light.

"Dang it," Zachary muttered.

"What?" Tonya asked quietly.

"No lights," Zachary answered.

"I'm scared," Brittany started to cry.

"Shhh," Tonya said to Brittany. She was scared, too, and didn't need Brittany reminding her. "What are we gonna do?" Tonya asked Zachary.

"We're gonna find Billy." Zachary took the flashlight from Tonya and turned it on.

"See? There it is," Natalie's voice came again. "Look. It's behind you."

Billy took a deep breath. He didn't want to take his eyes off them, but couldn't help himself. He looked over his shoulder with his flashlight still shining on the group.

His heart jumped into his throat. There was something behind him. A light. And it was coming straight for him.

Chapter 7

Billy turned and ran…from the light and from the group. He prayed to find his real cousins or a way out.

"Billy!" Zachary yelled.
"What's he doing?" Tonya asked as they began to run after him. "Billy!"
"Billy!" Brittany yelled through tears. "Stop!"

Billy smiled. He had found them. Doors to the outside. He was saved. He dropped the flashlight, and without stopping, pushed with both hands. The sweet sound of handles clanking and doors opening filled his ears. He stumbled through the doors and fell face down onto the sidewalk. Tears filled his eyes. He was safe.
"What the heck are you doing?" Zachary's voice came from behind him.
Billy gasped and rolled to his back. They had followed him outside the school.
"Why are you running from us?" Brittany asked, walking up to him.
"Get away!" Billy yelled. His heart pounded in his ears.
Brittany wiped the tears from her face. "What's wrong with you?"

"Why were you in the gym?" Tonya asked. "We're not supposed to wander off alone."

"It's really you." Billy slowly rose to his feet, the sound of his heart still in his ears.

"What?" the three asked in unison. They looked at each other.

"Oh man, when the lights went out, this thing was behind me. Then you guys were in front of me, but it wasn't you."

"The lights didn't go out," Zachary said. "You were in the gym. Those lights are out."

"No. I was going down the hall. I saw you guys setting up. Then something was behind me and the lights went…" He stopped and stared at the doors he had fallen out of. They were the gym doors. "I did not go into the gym." He hadn't, had he?

"Well, it doesn't matter now. We've got things set up. Let's get our proof and get out of here," Zachary said.

"Yeah," Tonya agreed. "Let's just get this done."

Billy nodded, but he didn't want to go back in there. Not with that thing. It was out to get him.

Brittany pulled on the door handles. "It's locked. Only opens from the inside."

"Guys," Tonya spoke into the walkie-talkie, "we're outside the gym. Locked out."

"Did you find Billy?" Samantha asked.

"Yeah," Tonya answered. She turned to Billy. "You still got the key, right?"

"Yeah, but it only opens Mom's door."

"We're on our way," Tonya said into the walkie-talkie, leading the way to the kindergarten room. "At least we came out those doors and not the ones on the other side."

Billy slid the key into the lock and opened the door. "We need to go back to the gym."

"What? Why?" Brittany asked. She didn't want to go back into that dark, scary place. She wanted to go home to her mom and dad where she was safe.

"My flashlight's in there and so is my duffel bag with the extra batteries *and* Mom's cell phone." He didn't want to go back in there either, but he didn't have a choice. Batteries and a flashlight were one thing, but his mom's cell phone…he refused to even imagine going home without *that*.

They slowly approached the gym doors.

"I don't want to go in there," Brittany said.

"I'll wait out here with Brittany," Tonya offered.

Zachary rolled his eyes. *Girls.* "Come on, Billy." He pulled the walkie-talkie from Tonya's hand. "In case we need to call for backup."

"No." Brittany was frantic. "You don't have to go in there. We can come back tomorrow when it's daylight and get it. It'll still be there."

"When I get the cell phone," Billy pulled the door open, "I'll call Mom and you can go home." He turned and followed Zachary into the darkness.

Chapter 8

Brittany and Tonya anxiously waited outside the gym.

Brittany leaned back against the wall, struggling to keep her eyes on the floor. She didn't want to peer through the small, door windows and into the darkness – she might see something she didn't want to see, but she wanted to know what was going on.

Tonya paced in front of the doors, glancing into the dark room each time she passed by the windows. "They'll be fine," she said.

"Shouldn't they be back by now?" Brittany asked, chewing on a fingernail.

Tonya stopped pacing. "Mmm. I don't think so. It's pretty dark in there," she answered. "It'll take 'em a little while." She started pacing again.

"They should've just waited until tomorrow," Brittany muttered.

"What?" Tonya asked.

"Nothing," Brittany replied, and began to chew on another fingernail. She still thought they should've been back by now.

Tonya stopped in front of the window and stared into the gym.

"What is it?" Brittany asked.

"They're coming."

"Really?" Brittany jumped beside Tonya and looked through the window. A beam of light was bouncing toward them.

"I told you they'd be okay," Tonya said.

Zachary popped through the doors first and handed the walkie-talkie to Brittany.

"What took you so long?" she asked.

"It didn't take us that long," Zachary replied.

Billy opened the duffel bag. "I'll call Mom. You can go home now."

"I don't want to go home now," Brittany said. Although she was still scared, she was starting to feel a little better.

Billy studied her a moment. "Okay. You can stay." He zipped up the bag and headed down the hall.

"I'll take that now." Tonya smiled at Zachary and slipped the flashlight from his hand. "Thank you."

"Hey, you made it," Andrew yelled as Billy, Zachary, Tonya, and Brittany approached.

"We're ready," Jessie said.

"I'm bored." Samantha rose from her seated position on the floor. "Do you ever see or hear anything?"

"So what happened?" Jessie asked. "Why were you in the gym?"

"Let's just get started," Billy answered. He would tell them about it later. His experience didn't get the evidence that they needed. "CJ...Valerie," Billy spoke into the walkie-talkie, "turn on your camcorders and digital recorders and bring your groups to the third grade pod."

"I'll turn ours on," Zachary said and jogged down to the second grade pod.

"What are we gonna do now?" Samantha asked.

"When they get here, we're gonna kill the lights and wait a couple hours in Mom's room. Then we'll walk around with the thermal scanner guns to see if there's a change in temperature. And then we'll get the digital recorders and start walking around asking questions to see if we get any answers."

"What happened?" CJ asked as he and the rest of the ghost hunters joined the group in front of the third grade pod.

"Yeah, what happened?" Valerie echoed CJ.

"We'll talk about it later," Billy replied. "Andrew go ahead and turn your recorders on and we'll shut the lights off with the main breaker."

Andrew turned them on, and the group started down the hall.

"Were you scared?" Chance asked Billy.

"No," Billy lied. He was too embarrassed to admit that he was scared. He was their leader and shouldn't get scared.

"I would've been," Ryan said.

"Yeah, me too," Chance said.

"Well, we're older," Natalie said. "We don't get scared that easy."

Just then, the lights went out. Everyone stopped in mid-stride.

Natalie grabbed Ryan's arm. "Why did the lights go off?"

"I thought you didn't get scared so easy," Ryan whispered. How was he supposed to not be scared when the older kids were getting scared?

Tonya turned her flashlight on. "It's probably just a fuse or something." She hoped.

CJ, Josh, and Jessie turned on their flashlights.

"Yeah, I'm sure that's it," Billy said, but didn't believe it. It was *them*. He was sure of it.

Chapter 9

"Stay together," Billy ordered, turning on his flash-light. "Walk slowly."

Valerie snapped a picture.

"What was that?" Billy asked, glancing over his shoulder.

"Me," Valerie answered, taking another picture. "I've got Mom's camera."

"Warn us next time," Joshua said, rubbing his eyes, blinded from the bright flash.

"Okay, sorry," Valerie said. "I'm taking another picture." She stopped, turned, and snapped a picture of the hallway behind them. As the flash lit up the space, she saw a little girl cross the hall from left to right. "Uh, Billy, I think I found your little girl."

"Really?" Jessie stopped. "Where?" She joined Valerie at the back of the group, shining her light down the hall.

"Turn off your light." Valerie waited for Jessie to turn her flashlight off. "Now watch." She snapped another picture.

Everyone stopped and turned to watch for the ghostly girl.

The little girl crouched down and lowered her face.

"I saw her!" Jessie yelled excitedly. She couldn't believe that she finally got to see the thing that had scared Billy so badly when they were in third grade.

"I'm taking another picture," Valerie warned.

The flash lit up the hall. The girl was gone.

"She's gone," Valerie announced.

"Good," Billy sighed, "Let's get to Mom's room."

They set the flashlights on the small desks, shining the lights up at the ceiling to light the room as much as possible.

"Was that really the little girl you saw when you were in third grade?" Brittany asked. She was starting to get scared again.

"I don't know for sure," Billy replied. "It was too dark to tell." He knew it was her…it. He knew it was.

"Valerie, did you get a picture of it?" Billy asked.

Valerie looked at the pictures on the small, LCD screen. "No," she answered, disappointed.

"Let me see," Jessie said, taking the camera from Valerie.

"They're too dark to see anything," Valerie said.

"She's right," Jessie agreed. "Here." She handed the camera back to Valerie.

As Valerie took the camera, her finger hit the button, snapping a picture. "Oops." She laughed.

"So what did you get?" Jessie asked, also laughing.

Valerie raised the camera and looked at the picture. "It's us," she replied, then looked at the picture again, studying it this time. "But not us."

"What?" Billy's heart began to race.

28

"It's us," Valerie explained. "But we're not standing like that."

Billy grabbed the camera from Valerie and looked at the picture. It was *them*. "They're in here with us."

"Who?" Jessie asked.

Billy gave the camera back to Valerie and gazed around the room. "They're in here with us," he stated again. "Take another picture."

Valerie raised the camera, pointing it at the door to the outside, and pushed the button. She showed Jessie and Billy the picture. It was *them* again. This time they looked angry. Valerie leaned against her aunt's desk. "We can't use this as proof, can we?"

"No, it's us," Billy replied.

"We need to tell the others," Jessie said, watching them as they relaxed and quietly talked, waiting for the couple hours to pass. "You guys, come here."

"What is it?" Natalie asked.

"Is it time to go?" Samantha asked.

"No, it's not time to go," Billy answered. "We've got something. Look."

They huddled around and passed the camera for everyone to see.

"This isn't really us," Josh said.

"No, it's not," Jessie confirmed.

"What does that mean?" Brittany asked, moving into the middle of her cousins.

"It means…it's in here with us," Tonya answered.

"Where?" Chance's eyes darted around the room.

"Everybody get behind the desk and back into the corner," CJ ordered.

Everyone did as he said—it sounded like a good idea to them. Chance and Ryan were side-by-side against the corner. Samantha, Brittany, and Natalie stood in front of them. Valerie, Zachary, Tonya, and Joshua were in front of them. And CJ, Billy, Jessie, and Andrew stood between them and the teacher's desk.

"Give me the camera." Jessie turned sideways and took the camera from Valerie. She pointed it at the rows of children's desks and pushed the button.

The pictured showed *them* in small groups around the five flashlights. Their eyes dark like death.

"They're gonna drain the flashlights," Billy said.

One light went out.

Jessie handed the camera to Billy. "Keep taking pictures."

"What are you gonna do?" Billy asked.

"I'm gonna get the flashlights and your bag with the batteries," she replied.

"No." Andrew grabbed her arm. "I'll go."

Another light went out.

"Maybe we should both go," Jessie said.

"I'll go," CJ said.

Another light went out. There were only two lights left shining.

"We'll all three go," Jessie decided. "And we need to go now before we're left in the dark."

"I'm ready." Billy pointed the camera at the desks. "Go."

Jessie, Andrew, and CJ ran for the flashlights with Jessie leading. She ran for the farthest light, one of the two still brightly shining, and the duffel bag of batteries. She grabbed them up and turned. Andrew and CJ had the four remaining flashlights, one in each hand, and were running back to the group huddled behind the teacher's desk.

The flashlight in CJ's right hand dimmed and went out.

Now Jessie had the only light left shining, and she was standing at the back of the classroom. She darted for the teacher's desk, keeping her eyes on the floor to avoid being blinded by the camera's flash.

"Come on, Jessie," Valerie called out. "You're almost here."

Jessie looked up as she approached the desk. She had made it. As she sat the bag on the desk, her light went out. She had barely made it.

Billy snapped another picture. It was Jessie, the real Jessie...with the thing hovering behind her! "Jessie!" He reached for her, but it was too late.

The thing grabbed Jessie around her throat and jerked her backwards. The flashlight fell from her hand. It landed on the desk with a clank, rolled across the desktop, and crashed to the floor.

Chapter 10

"What happened?" Valerie screamed. "Jessie?" Tears filled her eyes.

"It got her!" Billy yelled. He set the camera on the desk and dug into the duffel bag to find the batteries. "Grab a flashlight," he commanded, finding one himself. "Here." He shoved some batteries at them then opened his flashlight, dropped the dead batteries to the floor, and slid three new ones in.

"I'm scared," Brittany cried.

"I wanna go home," Chance said.

"Me, too." Ryan clung to Natalie's arm.

"Just be quiet." Billy pushed the button on the flashlight…nothing. He opened the flashlight and dumped the batteries to the floor.

"These batteries are dead, too." Valerie started to cry. "How are we gonna find Jessie?"

Billy picked up the camera. "When the camera's flash lights up the room, try to see if she's still in here." He snapped a picture. The room lit up for a brief moment. "Did anybody see her?"

"No," they answered.

"Now what?" Valerie asked. "We have no lights. How are we gonna find her in the dark?"

"I don't know," Billy answered. "I guess we can use the camera's flash…I just don't know."

"Hey," CJ jumped in, "I think there's a flashlight in the van. I'll go get it."

"I'll go with you," Andrew volunteered. He couldn't let CJ go alone. Something could happen to him.

Chance pushed his way to CJ. "I wanna go with you," he said, grabbing CJ's arm.

"We're coming back. You can't stay outside by yourself." CJ pulled away from him. "We'll be right back. Everything's gonna be okay."

Andrew and CJ slowly walked toward the door, feeling their way past the desks, silently hoping the thing was gone.

"There's a light!" Tonya exclaimed.

They had all seen it at the same time…a light shining through the door's window.

CJ and Andrew stopped, only three steps from the door.

Tap! Tap! Tap! Came from the glass.

CJ eased up to the door and peaked through the window. "It's Jessie's boyfriend, Jake," CJ announced and unlocked the door.

"What's going on?" Jake asked as he stepped into the room.

"Jessie's missing!" Valerie cried, approaching him.

"She's missing? How?"

"This is how," Billy replied, showing him the picture on the camera's tiny screen. "It got her."

Jake shined his light around the room. Jessie was nowhere in sight. "Where do you think it took her?"

"We'll be right back," CJ broke in. "We're gonna need more than one light." He and Andrew ran out the door.

Billy shrugged. "I don't know. Maybe it took her to the gym."

"Maybe it took her to the third grade pod," Zachary offered. "Isn't that where you saw it when we were in third grade?"

"Yeah," Billy answered, the memory sweeping over him.

"Maybe that's where it died."

Zachary's statement sent a chill up Billy's spine as he drifted back to that day.

Run, the voice inside him had yelled as he stood face-to-face with the ghost child, his eyes locked in an unwilling stare with its empty, dark eyes.

It grabbed his left wrist.

Its touch was icy cold. He tried to scream, but couldn't. His scream was caught in his throat. He struggled against its grip, but it was too strong! He couldn't get away!

It rose from the floor…and rose…and rose, until it towered over him. Its bony fingers, still squeezed around his wrist, pulled his arm into the air. "William." A whisper filled his ears.

Standing on tiptoes, arm stretched high above his head, he managed a tiny squeal, "Help."

But no one heard him. No one would be coming to save him.

It started floating away from the third grade pod, pulling him along.

He couldn't fight it! He was on tiptoes! How could he fight when he was dangling from its hand like a rag doll being carried away by its owner?

He reached for the walls...for anything that he could grab and hold on to, to keep from being taken away, but found nothing as he slid along the floor toward the second grade pod...then past the second grade pod, to the right...then right again and into the lunchroom.

"Let's go," Jake said, his voice shaking Billy from the terrifying memory. "I'll search the whole school if I have to."

"You won't have to," Billy said, breaking into a sweat. "It took her to the lunchroom."

Chapter 11

"Are we ready?" CJ asked as he and Andrew came back into the room. He held the shining flashlight in his left hand and locked the door with his right.

Billy took a deep breath and gazed around the group huddled in front of the door. "Yeah, I guess we are."

"I'm not going," Samantha said.

"I don't want to, either." Ryan held Natalie's arm.

"Maybe the younger kids should stay here," Natalie suggested.

"We have to stay together," Billy replied.

"I'm going with CJ." Chance grasped the back of CJ's shirt.

CJ smiled at Chance and patted his back. "I'll protect ya."

"What happens if it drains the batteries again?" Joshua asked.

Jake pulled a lighter from his pocket. "I'll use this."

Brittany stepped up to Billy. "I'm scared. I wanna go home."

"We can't go until we get Jessie," Billy replied.

"Call Mom." Brittany started to cry. "She can come and get me."

"No. We have to find Jessie first."

"I'll call her myself." Brittany walked over to her mom's desk and dug into the duffel bag. "She'll know what to do." She found the cell phone and pulled it out of the bag.

"You can't." Billy grabbed the phone from Brittany's hand. "We have to do this ourselves."

"What if it gets us, too?" Brittany cried.

"It wants me," Billy answered.

"What? Why?" Brittany asked.

"I don't know," he replied.

"Then, how do you know it wants you?" she asked.

"I just do." Billy turned around. They were all watching him—waiting for the answer.

Chapter 12

"What?" Billy asked the silent, staring group.

"If it wants you, why did it take Jessie?" Valerie asked.

"For bait, I guess," Billy answered.

"But, why?" Valerie didn't understand. "It could've taken you when it took Jessie, so why didn't it? If it wants you."

"I don't know." Billy shrugged. He didn't know what to tell them. Why didn't it take him? She was right. It could've taken him instead of Jessie.

"It doesn't matter," Jake said. "Let's go."

"Everybody stay together." Billy took the lead beside Jake.

"I'll take the back," Andrew offered.

"Me, too." CJ fell in line at the rear with Andrew as they marched out of the classroom.

With one light in front and one in back, they carefully made their way down the dark hallway to the lunchroom door.

"Stay together," Billy whispered, slowly pushing the door open.

They quietly entered the lunchroom.

"Jessie?" Jake whispered, calling for his girlfriend. "Jessie?" He shined his light under the lunch tables and around the room. "Where is she?" he questioned Billy.

"In there." Billy stared at the door to one of the rooms inside the lunchroom that was used for Music and Art.

Jake ran to the door and burst into the room. "Jessie!" he exclaimed.

Everyone ran in after him.

Jessie was sitting in the corner across the room. Her eyes closed; her head resting back against the wall. Her feet were stretched out in front of her. Her arms were down to her sides with the back of her hands resting on the floor.

Jake raced across the room and dropped to his knees beside her. "Jessie?" Tears came to his eyes.

"Is she…" That last word caught in Valerie's throat. She couldn't say it. She didn't want to think it, but her sister was sitting lifeless in the corner of a dark room. What else could she think?

"I knew we should've called Mom," Brittany cried.

Jake slipped his hand behind Jessie's neck and gently lifted her head.

"What's that smell?" Tonya asked, smelling the air. "Is it smoke?"

"They were in the lunchroom eating when the fire started," Zachary said.

"Who?" Natalie asked.

"All the kids were eating lunch when the fire started." Zachary's voice was soft, drifting through the air as if it were seeping through from the past. "The teachers rounded them up and led them out of the building. All of them, but four. They were here…in this room. They were scared and crying. No one came for them. No one saved them. They died, each in a corner…all alone."

Chapter 13

"Shut up, Zachary," Natalie said. "You're scaring me."

Jessie gasped. Her eyes sprung open. She gazed around the dark room. "Where are they?" she asked frantically. "We have to find them!"

"Who?" Jake asked.

"The kids." She pushed him back and rose from the floor. "Their teacher left without them."

"Jessie." Valerie rushed over to her sister. "Are you okay? What did it do to you?"

"I'm fine," Jessie answered. She sighed and looked into her boyfriend's eyes. "We have to find those kids."

"They're not real," Jake answered.

"What?" she asked, confused.

"Do you remember what happened?" Billy asked.

"There were four kids crying. They were standing in the corners," Jessie replied.

"Do you remember being in my mom's class-room?" Billy asked.

Jessie thought for a moment. "Yeah." She swallowed. "Oh, my God." She sat down on a desk. "It got me."

"What did it do to you?" Billy had to know. He had to know what it wanted.

"It—"

"We have to get outta here," Tonya broke in. "I smell smoke. Don't you smell it?"

"I smell it," Brittany said, running to the door. She grabbed the doorknob, turned, and pulled. "It won't open!" she yelled.

"What!" Billy ran to Brittany's side, followed by the rest of the group. He grabbed the knob. It turned, but the door wouldn't budge.

"It wanted us in here so it could trap us," Joshua said. "These are the only rooms without windows."

"Uh…guys." CJ shined his light at the bottom of the door.

Smoke poured through the space between the door and the floor.

"We're going to die like those kids!" Brittany yelled through tears.

Chapter 14

"No, we're not!" Billy shouted. He refused to believe that they were going to die. There had to be a way out. It just couldn't be the end for them.

"Then, how are we gonna get out?" Brittany asked.

"I don't know," Billy replied. He turned to the others. "Any ideas?" He hoped one of them had an idea.

"They want us to stay," Jessie said.

"Yeah...they want us to die like they did," Brittany said.

"They want us to save them," Jessie countered.

"How are we supposed to save them?" Valerie asked. "They're dead."

"That smoke is weird," Tonya announced. "We should be choking on it." She put her hand on the door. "The door's not hot."

"The only way out is to do what they want," Jessie said.

"How do you know what they want?" Billy asked.

"I can see them."

"Where?" The hair stood up on the back of Billy's neck...and everyone else's. They slowly huddled together.

"They're in the corners," Jessie replied.

Jake and CJ shined their lights into the corners. They were empty.

"Jessie, are you okay?" Jake asked. "Did you hit your head?"

Jessie gave her boyfriend a harsh look. "Just because you can't see them, doesn't mean something's wrong with me."

"Why can you see them and we can't?" Valerie asked.

"Because they want me to," Jessie answered. "Do you wanna know what it did when it took me?"

Billy nodded.

"It told me what it wanted." She stopped.

Billy swallowed. "What does it want?"

"It wants four of us," Jessie replied. "It needs four of us to set it free. It isn't an It. They're the four children."

"Who does it want?" Tonya asked.

"It wants Billy…and three of us to volunteer," Jessie said. "I'll volunteer…Will you?"

Chapter 15

"No!" Tonya scowled.

"Nobody's volunteering," Jake said.

"I will." Jessie gave Jake a stern look. "They need us."

"The smoke stopped!" CJ yelled, his flashlight lighting up the bottom of the door. He grabbed the knob and pulled. He shook his head. The door still wouldn't open.

"They'll open it, if there's one person in each corner," Jessie said.

"Fine," Billy said. "I'll do it." He searched the others' faces. "We need two more."

They looked at each other, waiting for someone to volunteer.

"Listen," Billy started, "all we have to do is stand in the corners. When the door opens, we can all leave."

"Okay," CJ said. "I'm in."

"Fine, I will too," Valerie reluctantly volunteered.

Jessie stood in the corner nearest the door. This corner would be behind the door once it opened. Billy took the other corner that shared the wall with the door. Valerie moved to the corner opposite of Jessie. And CJ was in the last corner, across from Billy.

Andrew tried the door. "It won't open," he announced.

"Face the corners," Jessie instructed.

Billy wasn't sure about turning his back to the room, but did it anyway.

The door creaked open.

"Come on! Let's go!" Jake grabbed Jessie's arm and tried to pull her around the door as the others ran out.

"What's going on?" Valerie yelled. "Jessie, I can't move."

"Me, either!" Billy struggled to move, but his feet were glued to the floor.

CJ pushed against the wall trying to free himself. "It won't let us go!" He twisted his upper body to see the others. Everyone, except the four in the corners and Jake, were standing outside the door. Jake tugged on Jessie's arm.

"Ow, let go." Jessie jerked her arm back. "You have to go out."

"I'm not leaving," Jake replied.

The door slammed shut.

"Billy! Jessie! Valerie! CJ! Jake!" the others yelled, banging against the door.

Jake ran to the door. "It won't open."

A hand came down on Jake's shoulder. He froze. He knew it wasn't Jessie or Valerie or Billy or CJ. He knew it was...*them*.

They pushed him forward, against the door, pulled him back, and then pushed him through the door. He fell to the floor.

"How did you do that?" Zachary asked, helping Jake to his feet.

"*They* pushed me through the door." Jake shined his light on the unbroken door.

"But, how did you go through the door…Are you dead?" Zachary backed away from him.

Chapter 16

"No, I'm not dead," Jake replied.

"We have to call Mom," Brittany blurted out. "She'll know what to do."

"Now that we have a light, we can get outta here," Tonya said.

"We can't leave them." Jake was firm. He would *not* leave Jessie…not even for a minute.

"We can't save them, either," Tonya countered. "We need to get help."

"What was that?" Jake shined his light at the lunchroom entrance.

Trinity was standing in front of the closed doors. She smiled. "I can help."

"That's not Trinity." Zachary stared at his little sister. "I can see right through her."

"It's me. TT." Trinity started toward them. She seemed to be gliding more than walking.

"Astral projection," Tonya said.

"What?" Jake asked.

"She's astral projecting." Tonya paused, waiting to see if they knew what she was talking about.

"Huh?" Samantha asked.

"She left her body," Tonya explained.

Trinity glided to the classroom door. "I can go in."

Zachary grabbed for his sister, but his hand swiped only air. "No!"

Trinity turned and faced him.

"Go home," Zachary commanded.

She shook her head, and walking backwards, disappeared into the door.

"How can she help them?" Zachary thought out loud. "She's only four years old."

"I don't know," Tonya answered. "But you can't make her go home."

"She—" Zachary stopped. The classroom doorknob was slowly turning.

Jake's light jumped to the door as it slowly creaked open, white smoke pouring out.

They all stared and watched, waiting for someone to emerge from the smoke-filled room.

Jake took a deep breath. He couldn't wait any longer. He had to go in to see if they were ok. He darted through the doorway…and disappeared into the smoke.

Chapter 17

"Trinity?" Billy stared in disbelief.

"I'm here. Let's play," Trinity said.

"Trinity?" CJ turned. He was free. "What are you doing here?" He could barely see her. He turned the flashlight on. He still couldn't see her very well through the smoke.

"Come on." Trinity stood in the middle of the room.

"How did you get here?" CJ walked up to her.

"She's not here," Jessie said, joining CJ and Trinity.

"What do you mean?" Valerie asked, making her way to the middle of the room.

"Look," Jessie pointed at Trinity. "You can see through her."

"Is it really her?" Billy asked.

"She's astral projecting," Jessie replied.

Trinity pointed to the doorknob. It slowly turned. The door creaked open. "Go," she commanded. "I'll save the children."

"How are you going to save the children?" Billy asked.

"I have to show them how to get out," Trinity replied.

Jake burst through the smoke and bumped into Jessie. "Are you okay? What's going on?"

"Yeah, I'm okay," Jessie replied. "Trinity's here."

"I know," Jake said.

"You have to go now." Trinity backed away from them. She stood against the far wall.

Natalie watched the others watch the doorway. No one was coming out. What were they waiting for? "Should we go in?" Natalie asked, breaking the silence.

"What for?" Samantha countered.

"I don't know if we should." Tonya looked to the others.

Andrew slowly approached the room and peaked inside.

"Well?" Tonya asked.

"I can't really see anything," Andrew replied. "It's too dark and smoky. But, I do see a flashlight."

"Billy?" Brittany called out as she eased up to the doorway. "Do you think they're okay?" she whispered to Andrew.

Andrew shrugged. "There's only one way to find out." He stepped into the room.

Chapter 18

Andrew walked up to his cousins standing in the middle of the room. "What's going on?" he asked.

"Trinity," Jessie replied.

Andrew looked across the room. Trinity was standing against the wall. Four ghostly children stood beside her, two on each side.

"Go now," Trinity commanded.

"Come on," Jessie encouraged everyone. "It's time to get our stuff and go."

"I can't leave Trinity with *them*," CJ said.

"It'll be okay," Jessie said. "She's not physically here, anyway."

Trinity and the children turned, putting their backs to the group. Trinity took the hands of the two children beside her, and they took the hands of the two children beside them.

"Trinity, no!" Zachary yelled as Trinity and the children stepped up to the brick wall and disappeared into it.

"Come on!" Billy exclaimed. "Let's get the stuff and get outta here."

"She'll be okay," Jessie encouraged.

The lights began to flicker.

"What's going on?" Brittany asked. She grabbed Billy's arm.

"I don't know," Billy replied, shaking her off. "Let's just get the stuff and go."

They ran out of the lunchroom and took a right. Valerie grabbed the bag and the camcorder that her group had setup in front of the first grade pod and followed the others up the few steps to retrieve the camcorder that was setup by CJ's group. The lights continued to flicker.

"Why are the lights flickering?" Valerie asked Jessie as they ran back down the stairs and headed for the second grade pod to collect the equipment there.

"I don't know," Jessie replied. "Trinity's taking the children out. The lights should be on…Maybe they're not completely gone, yet."

Billy grabbed the bag and stuffed the camcorder inside it, then caught up with the others at the third grade pod. "Let's get the stuff from my mom's room and get the heck outta here."

The lights stopped flickering and came on.

"They must be gone," Jessie said.

They all ran down the hallway, past the lunchroom—glancing inside as they passed by—and entered the kindergarten room where they had started.

They filled the bags with all the equipment.

"Should we turn all the lights off?" Natalie asked.

"We'll turn this one off," Billy answered, walking over to the door with the others right behind him. He was glad to be leaving. He put a hand on the doorknob and took a deep breath as he started to turn it. The night was finally over.

"Come on." Samantha began to grow impatient. How long did it take to open a door?

Billy slowly turned to his cousins. "I can't open the door."

Chapter 19

"What?" Brittany exclaimed.

Andrew stepped up to the door. "It's locked," he laughed.

Billy's face grew hot. He felt so stupid. He laughed nervously as he unlocked the door. He hoped that would do it.

He twisted the doorknob and pulled the door open. They were free.

Billy locked and shut the door after everyone had filed out. "Do you think they're gone for good?" he asked Jessie.

"Yeah, I think so," Jessie replied.

They loaded the equipment and climbed into their vehicles.

Billy took one last, long look at the building that had terrified him so. It was calm now. Peaceful. It no longer seemed alive.

"It's almost like it was a dream, isn't it?" Andrew asked as they drove away.

"Yeah," Billy replied as his mom's cell phone began to ring. He dug the phone out of his pocket and answered it. "Hello?…Yeah, we're on our way home."

His face turned white. "What?" His voice trembled. "What do you mean she's missing?"

Chapter 20

"Okay, we're on our way. Bye." Billy turned the cell phone off. He looked at Andrew. "Trinity's missing."

"Should we go back?" Andrew asked.

"No. Let's just go to Grandma's like we planned. When we get there, we'll tell the others before we go inside."

Billy and Andrew parked on the side of the road behind Tonya. "Hey!" Billy yelled to them. "Come here!"

The gang looked puzzled as they walked over to Billy and Andrew. "Trinity's missing," Billy said as they approached.

"What?" Jessie exclaimed. "She's missing? How do you know?"

"Mom called me on the cell phone," Billy answered.

"We have to go back to school," Zachary said.

"We need to look for her here. She may have been hiding when she left her body," Jessie explained.

"I think I know where she might be," Chance blurted out. "Come on!" He ran to the side door with everyone behind him. "It's locked!" He ran around the corner to the front door, ran through the livingroom, through the diningroom, through the kitchen, and up the stairs to his right. At the top of the stairs, he turned left and ran to the bedroom closet.

"What are you doing?" their grandma yelled after them.

Chance opened the closet door. On the left-hand side of the closet, hung a long dress. He pushed it aside, and there, on the little step behind the dress, was Trinity—curled up, sound asleep.

"Wait," Tonya whispered. "I don't think you're supposed to wake someone that's out of their body."

"What are you guys doing?" Grandma's voice came from the bedroom doorway.

They all jumped, their heads jerking toward the doorway.

"We—" Valerie started.

"Trinity!" Grandma exclaimed. Tears filled her eyes.

Trinity ran to Grandma and wrapped her arms around her neck.

"You had us scared to death." Grandma squeezed her tight. "We better tell your mom and dad that you're okay." She carried Trinity away from her cousins and down the stairs leaving the ghost hunting group with questions that would never be answered—for when asked later that night, Trinity had no memory of the events at the school or the ghostly children she had rescued them from.